I0760714

THE *Music* THAT MAKES ME *Dance*

THE *Music* THAT MAKES ME *Dance*

A Collection of Poetry

Beatrice Perry Soublet

CITIOFBOOKS, INC.
3736 Eubank NE Suite A1
Albuquerque, NM 87111-3579
www.citiofbooks.com
Hotline: 1 (877) 389-2759
Fax: 1 (505) 930-7244

Ordering Information:
Quantity sales. Special discounts are available on quantity purchases by corporations, associations, and others. For details, contact the publisher at the address above.

Printed in the United States of America.
ISBN-13: Hardcover 978-1-962366-05-2

Library of Congress Control Number: 2023916240

Dedication

I dedicate this collection of poems to the B Sharp Music Club, the historic more than a century-old organization of New Orleans' African American musicians Mrs. Leah Chase, a legendary creole chef, civil rights guardian and grand lady

Table of Contents

Home Ties

If she could do one thing—she'd go home.
And smell the rich smells of Cafe du Monde
And Dooky's oysters and gumbo
And remember what eternal
spring or summer was like
And watch the graceful banana trees
respond to gentle breezes
And know that the long, wide, deep, dark
bayou holds Marie Laveau's secrets still.
And see funeral second lines reflect
rejoicing for the escaped brother,
Marchers carrying umbrellas reminiscent
of those held over African royal
And touch Spanish moss which
makes trees shed gray tears;
And hear streetcars on old tracks humming
an old tune for four generations
If she could do one thing she'd go home.

Front Steps

Sitting here, we can see a myriad of beauty.
New buds on once dead trees.
New life amidst horror
We see what we remembered would come.
Years of experience with spring
Teach us to remember that hope and life come
from seemingly dead things.
Dreams long ago forgotten come back to us in
lucid moments
Clarity is the true gift.
Memory, her sister.
Dreams wait on life's front porch
For the return of hope.

Here's to You, B Sharp

I lift my glass to toast you
For your having survived.
And come through the Middle Passage
To touch these shores alive.

I raise my glass to toast you,
For having maintained in your heart.
The sound of your ancestors' drumbeat.
For that was the better part

For was it not through music,
The sorrow songs you wrote,
The horrors of slavery were vanquished
And God praised in every note?

And was it not your creative genius
That gave to this country its song?
And have you not preserved it
Throughout your history long?

And so to this organization the B Sharp Music Club.
I lift my glass to toast you in a city where culture's the hub.
For your century of efforts for causes both general and rare.
For musicales, scholarships and pleasant hours,
For years of just being there.

When in old segregated New Orleans, when our
places for culture were few
We could have our spirits encouraged by the noble
work that you'd do
For Miss Nickerson, Miss Hutton, Mr. Rousseve,
Mrs. Perry,
And all those who followed their lead
I salute you as modern-day liberators
For you truly our spirits have freed.

Mardi Gras People Those of Us Who Deserted

We drop in, run through
Steal the sweets
"Hey Mister, throw me something!"

Powdered sugar on beignets
Strong, strong coffee
Po-boys with shrimp fallin' off
Dressed oh yeah, dressed

We see the Bayou
The Lake
The clouds
We drink in the wonder, the beauty.

We leave you to your struggle
We leave you to figure out the news.
We leave you to believe in the levees
The harsh realities of everyday life.

We second line through your lives
We leave you to Laissez le Bon Temps Roulez
When the good times are few.

Sing It, Stevie

Lifting, swaying, rocking
To a rhythm that our hearts can't feel
Or hear until you give it to us

Seeing with darkened eyes
What our dead lights can only imagine.
Sing it, Stevie
And let your song fill this world and the next.
And turn the strident sounds of hatred
Into harmonious reverberations of
Love, joy and peace

Music

We played our loud music outside
As the bird sang its song
And our strident sounds were different
20 years after

But the brave bird still sang its lovely song
Too beautiful for mortal ears
But from the other side of the river
We heard it,
And our hearts were glad

Melody

You are a heartfelt rendition of an old song
Something we remember well
Something we can hum
A tune that rises in us like a tide at sunrise
You come in us with your melody and bring us joy

Mornings of joy
Sing to us again

Angel of light
Familiar melodies make our hearts at one

African Dancing

Honey, I ain't never gonna keep up with dat rhythm.
It goes too fast.
The drums have me spinning too quick.
I'm bim, bah, dee, dee, bim, bah, dee, dee, dee, dee,
bim bahing,
And the drums are sayin' tee, tee, ti, ti, tee, ti, ti, ti

Maybe if I stop thinkin 'bout ballet and modern and all
That ole stuff and move with a sense of rhythm
that must be
Somewhere in my remembrance, I'll get it.

Surely I know that drum beat.
It was the last thing I heard when I got here.
Lemme stop thinking 'bout steps and imitating
the person
In front of me and move with the beat of my heart
In rhythm with the beat of the drum,
In harmony with the pendulum in my head,
And lift up my African hips and wave my arms and just fly.

Music

For Eddie Jackson and the Ellington Concert Choir

I wonder, don't you,
Whoever heard in her heart
The first note, the first song,
The beginnings of the first melody?
Where was the rhythm moving before it moved in us?
When did it first come?
When did it form and why?
Who sounded that first wonderful note that
re-verberated throughout the universe?
Did it start in the heart of God?
Will it return there?

Sing

You can really sing
A clear unaltered voice
Straight tone
No tremelo

A young voice
No pain revealed
No valleys of woes

Just a clear voice
Tone quality perfect

Sing an old song
See if it brings out the dusky sound

Sing some blues
See if the tone changes
Sing a spiritual
See if we can hear your people sing through you

You can really sing.

Old Church Sister

Swayin' back and forth to an ageless rhythm
that only her heart remembers
"Amens "and "Yes Jesuses" explode and erupt
Like involuntary belches from her digestive system.

Then the body movements—
coming on, repetitive sacred,
Somehow reminiscent or those movements
Made by all of us in the throes of that high act of love.

Rock on, sister.
Sway us back to the age
Where our bodies spoke a language
From another world.

Life Book

What are you writing?
What does each pulsing
Beat of your heart record?

Do you carry too much
Of your yesterday with you
Like so much worn luggage?

Does yesterday crowd in
Robbing you of the sweetness of the morning?
To what tune do you dance?
Is there an anchor, a mooring?

Child's Song

How radiant their faces
So recently come from their Maker
They yet glow from His Brightness
And their singing echoes that of His angels
When God sings it is through children.

Love Music

I touched your small brown hands
And felt the pulsing of the music
That lives within you;

I watched your bright eyes and saw a dancing brook;
And then you smiled and the tempo of my heart
Quickened and moved with the rhythm of yours.

Untitled

So many longings ago,
A sadness crept across his heart,
Like a shadowy evening
Which enfolds the forest in its darkness,
Making it cold and mysterious,

He had become a dreary, bothersome person
Whose presence permeated a room
And turned a convivial evening into a mournsome night.

And she came,
And rained on and through him
With a warm, quick, spring rain
That bathes air and field alike
And his sadness left forever.

Love Bath

I've melted your voice and your smile
And put them in an earthen bowl
I pour them over me
And bathe in the luxurious warmth of your love.

Age

Hair once dark now light and shadowy
Faces still echo smiles now gone
But well remembered
Eyes blest to see what was and what is.

Voices still sing songs once sung in stronger tone
Hearts warmed by love received
Now enriched by love given
How gracious of God to give us age when we have
time to appreciate it.

Old Love

Sweet memories that grow dearer each day.
Today's glances that recall yesterday's solemn stares
A flame once burning still warms a heart that remembers.
No death for love only a change of circumstance.

Young Man

How fragile
How delicate your hold on life,
And our hold on you
Which one
Which two will not be
Will not last,
How can we know?
How can we be sure
That it will not be our own
As are they all?

The Good Life

I'm going to live to be 100 years old.
Come on, join me.
I'm gonna praise God everyday
Tell somebody I love 'em.
Say good mornin' and how ya doin' to people I never saw.
Stop lil' children from fussin' in the street.
Love me a sweet good man.
And if I die tomorrow, I'll proclaim myself
One hundred years old:
"Cause maybe bein' 100 years old is
Giving 100 percent of yourself to
Learn, live love and serve your people.

Rain

Fail gently sweet rain
And dampen our pride and cockiness
Crush our conceit with your tender bullets
That our true imperfections will be made known.

Fall gently sweet rain and beat out your rhythm
For my love and me
That we may find a rhythm of our own.

Unassembled

You sold me an unassembled piece of your life.
No directions came
"Some assembly required"
Stamped on your heart.

You brought me your brokenness
Expecting that I could mend you.

I sought a complete life
I longed for something that would fit
"No assembly required"

I longed for a piece that would not need to be
forced in place
My heart was open to receive it.

I found you at the center of my longing
Broken, unassembled, wanting,
And I loved you.

Harvest

Eating the harvest from your hands
You made it sacred
You made it holy
By sharing, by giving
You blessed it.

Grace was the fire in our hearts.
Our passions were cooled by love,
Sustained by a rich faith
We went out to give, share love.

We were the harvest
We were planted
We gave and grew.

Seed Time to Harvest

Somewhere in between the start of things
And their fruition
We lost our way
Forgetting what we had been promised if we
endured to the end

Forgetting what had been suffered,
We lost our way
Planted by those who labored,
Unseen by us, unknown
Seeds sown in bitter soil

Toil unrequested, unknown
Dispassionate managers
Overseers who were lazy, indolent ignoramuses

We who were not there for planting
Did not know how blood, sweat,
tears nourished the soil

We who did not plant lost our way
We took part in the fruit but only weakly
For we cannot know of planting time
We were not there and we do not force ourselves
And our children to remember

We eat the fruit from bitter planting
And our teeth are set on edge
We know not why
Those who sow in tears, weep in joy,
Not so

Standing at the Door

Blocked at every turn
Some unforeseen obstacles
Stopped by closed doors.

No way to get around and through
You give up and revert
to your old ways of being

Going backward
Not remembering history
Forgetting our ancestors
Those who were not stopped by closed doors.

A closed door is not locked
You are not locked out
Except in your imagination.
Knock and enter.

Protester

You stand outside,
Still shouting
Convinced that there is no seat at the table.

Your long memory,
Your ignorance
Your superstition,
Convince you that you will not be heard

Convinced that a closed door is a locked door,
You stand outside and yell.

You have not learned to collaborate, cooperate, listen

Convinced that a closed door is locked
You stand outside,
Shouting, too loud to hear the invitation to enter.

God Sends Angels

For Dr. Sumersill

God sends angels
Everyday in our lives
To save us from ourselves and others
And like opening windows in heaven
God's angels open windows in our hearts
And breathe the fresh, loving air of life into us,
And our world is never the same
God has called God's angel home.

Death

The sound of your voice is gone.
Rich, deep, resonant
Nothing more
Visual memories
Flashes from the end

Time traveler-you
Now gone from our realm,
Living in angelic wonder
Could we have bid you farewell?

Could we but send you on that journey?
What words are there?
How do we touch cold flesh?
Red-staring eyes?
How do we send you on that journey of no return?
So now we wait for healing
For a time when memories will not bring sadness but joy.
May our grieving be deep and wide, but not long.

Blended

We made a list of ingredients
A recipe for joy
We mixed them well
Used the correct temperature

Cooked for the right length of time
No more pain for us
We had the recipe
Used our culinary skills of kindness

Made our appetizers our smile
At the end, we came forward with a sumptuous dish of goodness
Blended our hope with the hope of the others like us
Made the lives of those who struggle, better
We used an old recipe
Found it in an old book
The one their parents read
The one whose main message our Brother spoke

Nature's Audience

You can stay inside
You can watch the flood, the wind
The sun will not burn you
The cold will not chill you

You are protected
You are the audience
You can watch the ice cap go
The rivers rise, the hurricane wind blow

You watch, you observe
an audience, unconcerned, untouched
you listen to reports
warming of the earth

changes natural you say a cycle
things will come around
you watch from your box seat

Nature's audience
Your applause muted
By the cries of the innocent

The Meadow

Judging from my reaction
You thought I was lost
Not so, only gone to my meadow
My grassy place that expands me.

My mind which opens to a park and
To a lake and to a stream

Find me a place that will broaden us
You and I find a place to expand you
To meet me at a giving place
Open a heart that is locked

A meadow is a place to start.

Uninvited Guests

We came
Not knowing the deceased
We wept on cue
Bowed our heads

Rocked in anguish
Keened with those who could
We did not know the dead one
We only knew death, so we knew what to say

We wept, we wailed, we waited
The sound of the casket closing quietly
The sound of others weeping
We found our meaning as uninvited funeral guests

Risen

Standing at the open tomb
We waited, we watched, fearful
Where was he?
How had he come to save us and left?

So cruelly treated
Crucified
We went on trembling feet
We looked in and saw the empty tomb.

What could we have felt, have known, have wondered?
"They have taken my lord away."

Not they-
God came and got God's child
After so much pain
And rocked him up to heaven

www.ingramcontent.com/pod-product-compliance
Lightning Source LLC
Chambersburg PA
CBHW030602310726
48979CB00003B/536

* 9 7 8 1 9 6 2 3 6 6 0 5 2 *